THE PARK-EONTOLOGIST

Dedicated to Dinosaur lovers everywhere
(especially Eden Rose and Landon)

—Scott

ISBN 13: 978-1-4621-4162-3

Published by Sweetwater Books, an imprint of Cedar Fort, Inc.
2373 W. 700 S., Springville, UT 84663
Distributed by Cedar Fort, Inc., www.cedarfort.com

Library of Congress Control Number: 2021940600

Cover design & typesetting by Shawnda T. Craig
Cover design © 2021 Cedar Fort, Inc.

Printed in the United States of America

10 9 8 7 6 5 4 3 2 1

Printed on acid-free paper

THE PARK–EONTOLOGIST

WRITTEN BY SCOTT T. E. JACKSON • ILLUSTRATED BY LINDA PELLICANO

SWEETWATER BOOKS • AN IMPRINT OF CEDAR FORT, INC. • SPRINGVILLE, UTAH

On a sunny day like any other,
I went to the park with my sister and mother.

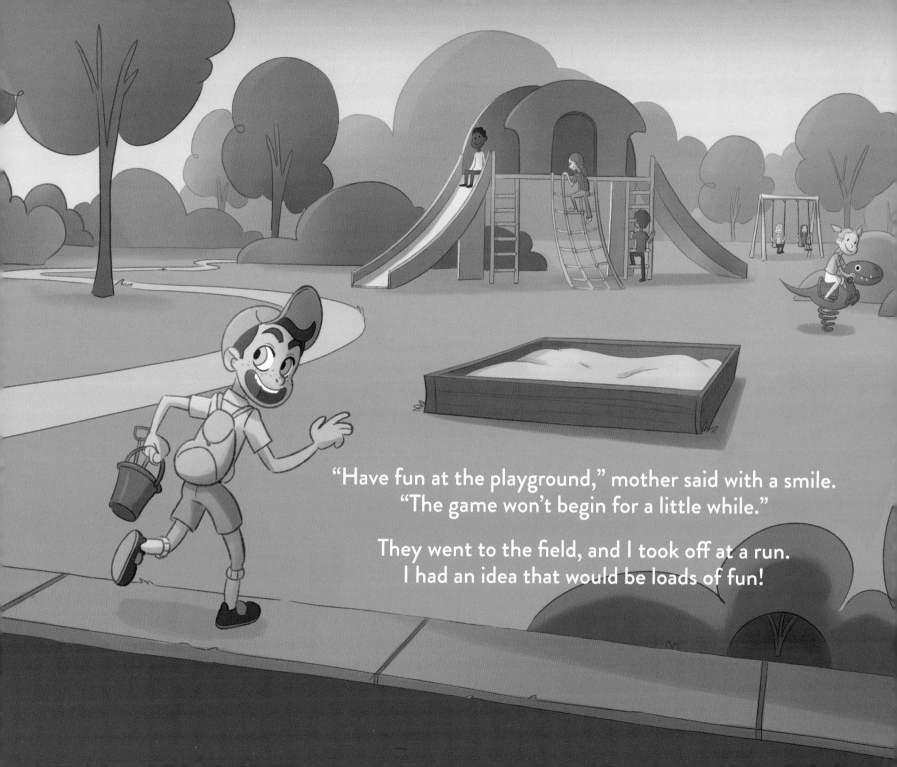

"Have fun at the playground," mother said with a smile.
"The game won't begin for a little while."

They went to the field, and I took off at a run.
I had an idea that would be loads of fun!

They call me the park-eontologist.
It's a long name, but I'll give you the gist:

I dig up old bones and study the features
Of dinosaurs and other prehistoric creatures.

FUN FACT: Paleontologists are grown up Park-eontologists and they do many of the same things.

In a flash, I arrived at my first dino-station,
And I began to dig like a happy Dalmatian.

The kids all around me stared in awe
As I pulled out a leg bone, a tooth, and a jaw!

FUN FACT: If you want to find your own Dinosaur fossils, just search in rock formations from the specific time period!

"This could be a Diplodocus or something much older."
Just then, I felt a tap on my shoulder.

A Dilophosaurus stood there with a curious look.
It's like he had walked off a page in my book!

FUN FACT: BiRDs are probably the only kinds of
Dinosaurs left alive . . . But, then you never know.

He chirped and he bobbed
and ran off with a flick.
I blinked and I shook.
Could this be a trick?

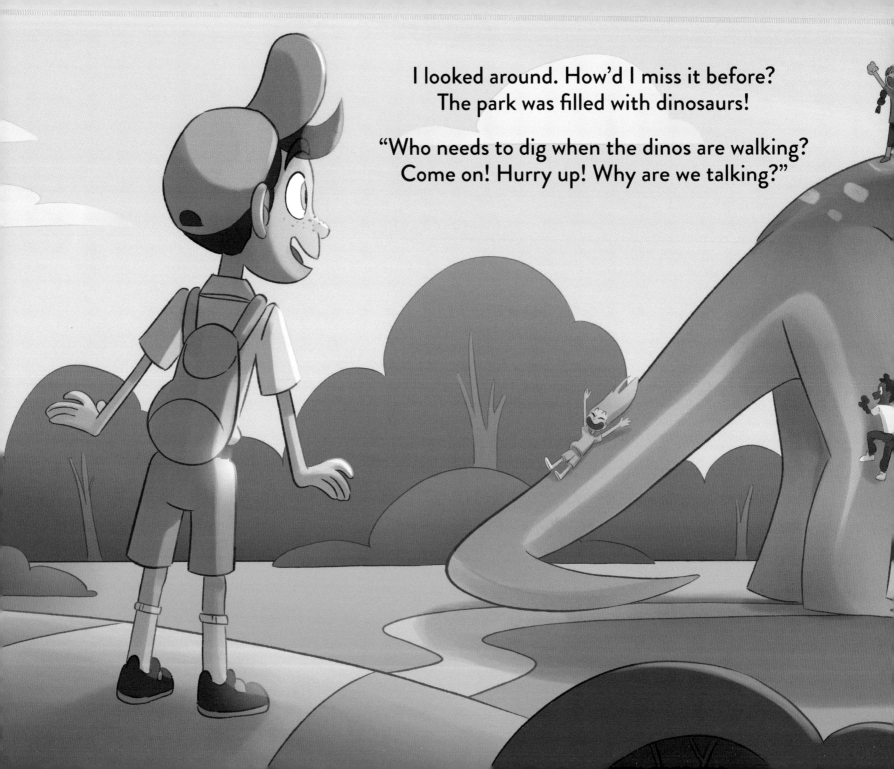

I looked around. How'd I miss it before?
The park was filled with dinosaurs!

"Who needs to dig when the dinos are walking?
Come on! Hurry up! Why are we talking?"

FUN FACT: Dinosaurs roamed the earth for over 165 million years!

Come slide down a sauropod.
There are dozens of choices:
Saltasaurus, Sonidosaurs, and
Supersaurs with bellowing voices.

The classic Apatosaurus will do fine for me,
So I wait my turn patiently.

FUN FACT: SAUROPODS included the largest land animals
that ever lived. Some were longer than Blue whales!

On the side of the herd, I see something new:
Raptors to ride! "I don't mind if I do!"

FUN FACT: Raptors are named after Birds of Prey (like hawks and eagles). Look at their claws for the resemblance!

I slid down the tail right into the saddle,
Though a raptor is a little scary to straddle.

The kids around me hopped on their theropod steeds,
And we were off to the races at a breakneck speed!

My ride seemed sweet despite his claws.
My Velociraptor kept running without even a pause!

FUN FACT: Velociraptors were small and fast and they may have hunted in packs like wolves do today.

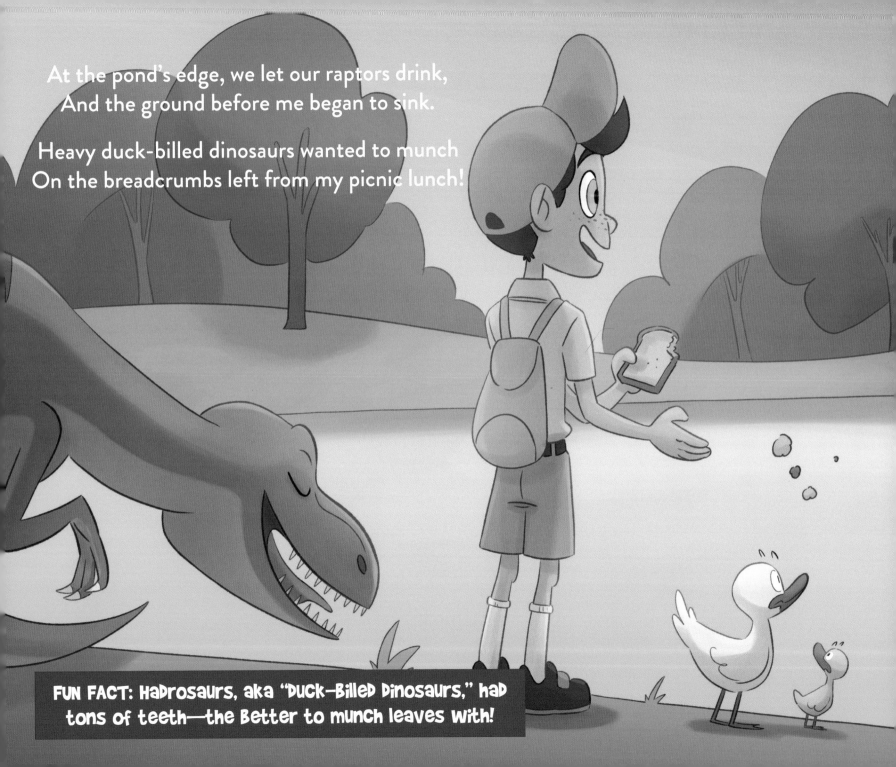

At the pond's edge, we let our raptors drink,
And the ground before me began to sink.

Heavy duck-billed dinosaurs wanted to munch
On the breadcrumbs left from my picnic lunch!

FUN FACT: HaDrosaurs, aka "Duck-Billed Dinosaurs," had
tons of teeth—the Better to munch leaves With!

I shared some with the ducklings till there was no more.
Nothing's as hungry as a fourteen-hundred-toothed Hadrosaur!

Dropping my last crust, I said, "See ya later."
I wouldn't want to get chomped by a prehistoric gator.

So I was off again down the path a bit
And was tagged with a roar—I was it!

I played tag with Gryposaurus, Gallimimus, Gastonia, and their friends. Even Gorgosaurus joined in, though not till the end.

FUN FACT: Some Dinosaurs were Built for speeD, others for attack, anD others for Defense. Can you tell which is which?

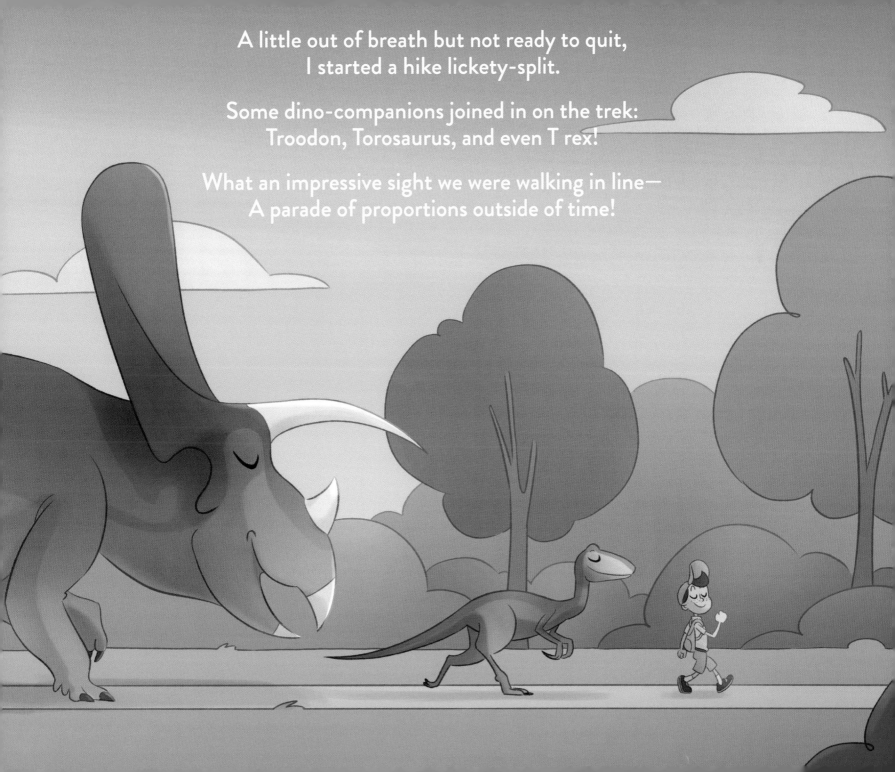

A little out of breath but not ready to quit,
I started a hike lickety-split.

Some dino-companions joined in on the trek:
Troodon, Torosaurus, and even T rex!

What an impressive sight we were walking in line—
A parade of proportions outside of time!

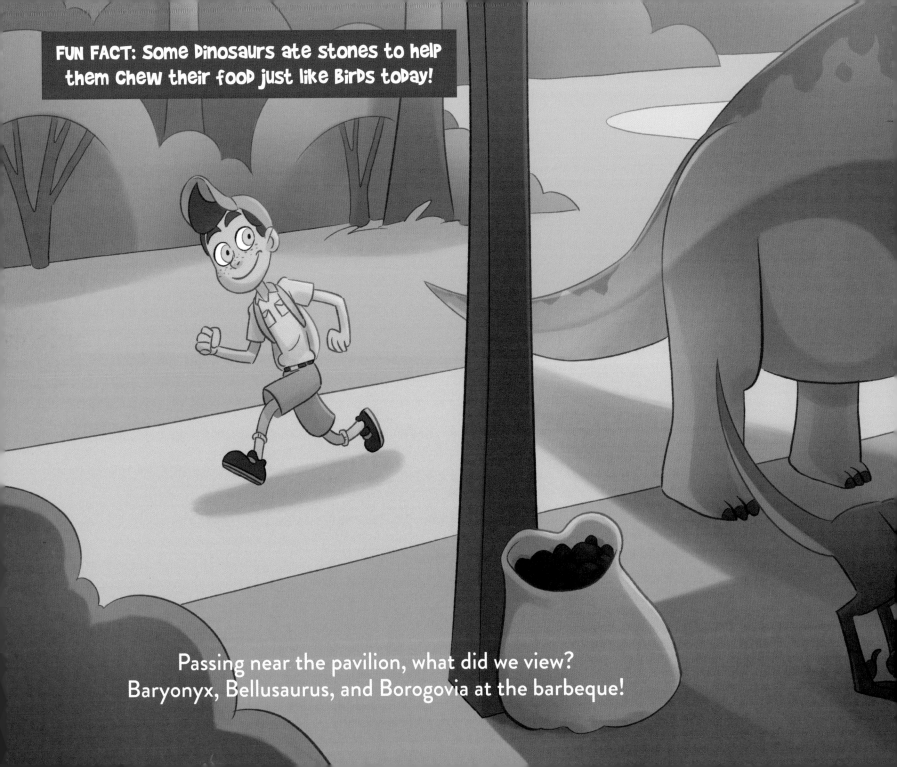

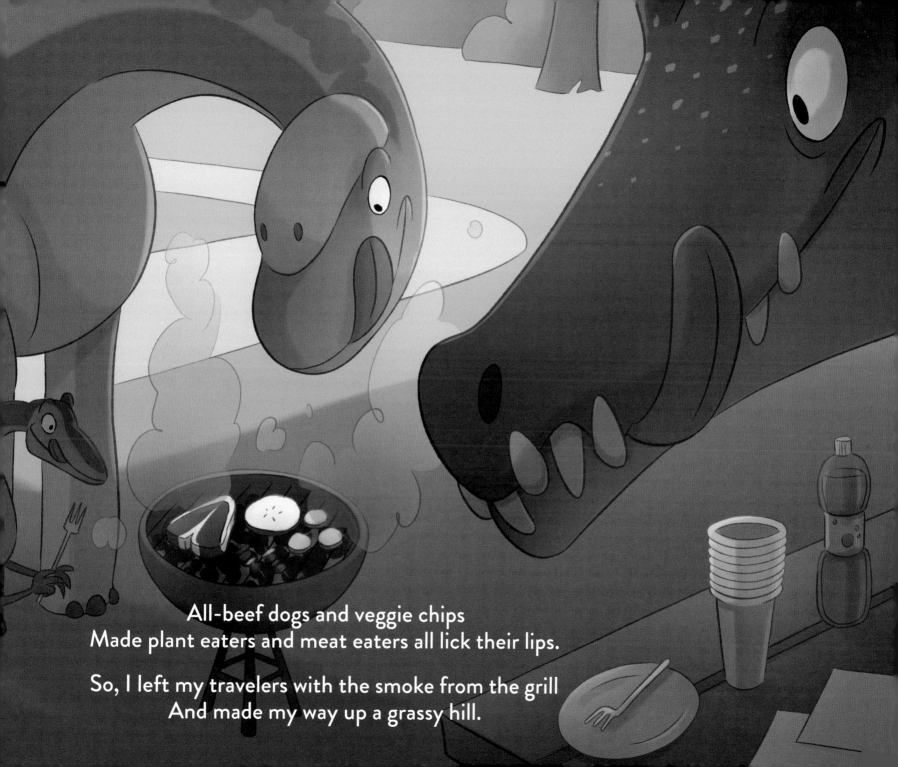

All-beef dogs and veggie chips
Made plant eaters and meat eaters all lick their lips.

So, I left my travelers with the smoke from the grill
And made my way up a grassy hill.

Suddenly, the world dropped off to the side.
A cliff was there that I'd never spied!

Although not a dinosaur, a fact I happily ignored,
I then got to fly with the pterosaurs!

Back and forth through the cerulean skies we swung
Like colorful boomerangs recently flung.

FUN FACT: Pterosaurs were cousins to Dinosaurs as
part of a larger family of reptiles called archosaurs.

But over the grass and the screams of glee,
I heard my mother calling for me.

FUN FACT: Quetzalcoatlus was the largest
Pterosaur and was the size of a small plane!

So, with one last swing, I leapt from the flying lizard's back.
I struck a landing and got ready to track.

I waved goodbye to each
new Mesozoic friend.
"I hope you'll be here when
I come back again!"

Thereafter I found mom and
sat down for the match
And wondered if they noticed
the "ball" starting to hatch!

FUN FACT: Some Dinosaur eggs were
really the size of soccer Balls!

PUT YOUR CHILD IN THE STORY!

Your child can slide down tails, play tag with the dinosaurs, and be the star of the story with their own customized children's book.

Create custom avatars that look like you and your child, insert your names, and instantly preview your custom book before it's printed and shipped right to your door.

Never before has a book been this cool!
Create your custom book today at **PERSONALIZE.CEDARFORT.COM**

CEDAR FORT
Publishing & Media